PET
SELECTOR!

words&pictures

RUSSELL KANE

PRESENTS...

PET
SELECTOR!

ILLUSTRATED BY
ERICA SALCEDO

words & pictures

© 2024 Quarto Publishing Group USA Inc.

Text © 2024 Russell Kane
Illustrations © 2024 Erica Salcedo

Russell Kane has asserted his right to be identified as the author of this work.
Erica Salcedo has asserted her right to be identified as the illustrator of this work.

First published in 2024 by words & pictures, an imprint of The Quarto Group.
100 Cummings Center, Suite 265D Beverly,
MA 01915, USA.
T (978) 282-9590 F (978) 283-2742
www.quarto.com

A CIP record for this book is available from the Library of Congress.

ISBN: 978-0-7112-9019-8

Manufactured in in Guangdong, China TT042024
9 8 7 6 5 4 3 2 1

FSC
www.fsc.org
MIX
Paper | Supporting
responsible forestry
FSC® C016973

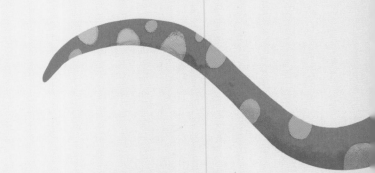

Dedication

Do I dedicate this book to a furry friend or a human? Hmm. Even that doesn't make much sense to me, as some of my favorite humans are furry (hiya, Auntie Carol) and some of my best animal friends had no hair at all . . . (You'll learn about my beloved stick insect Rambo later.)

Anyway—I had better thank my busybody, always supportive mom, JULIE, and my permanently moody bodybuilder dad, DAVE. My dad did not smile very often but he worked harder than any other dad I knew, and I felt safer than a tortoise with a double shell —so, Dad, thank you. I miss you. And a double thanks, to both of you, for ALWAYS saying YES to pets. Cats, dogs, insects, reptiles, and even jumping beans (Mexican beans with moth babies inside). My love of animals comes from my mom and dad trusting me to take care of my pets. I am as passionate today about pets as I was back then. I always will be. While we're talking about pets . . . ALBERT THE BURMESE, my first real love—I also dedicate this book to you.

I can't finish this page without thanking the Queen and Princess who have supported me and listened to all my words when I was test-reading. My beautiful wife, LINDSEY, and my darling, darling daughter, MINNA (rhymes with dinner). There is so much love in me bursting out all over the place—that's why my pets are important: they can absorb all that extra squish I have to let out!

RUSSELL X

HISTORY

The Abyssinian is so ancient that no one really knows its origins. The breed got its name because the first ones were brought to England from Egypt, after the Abyssinian war in the 1860s. There are also ancient Egyptian drawings of cats that seem to have the Aby's distinct reddish "ticked" coat. Genetic tests, however, suggest that the Aby may have originated in India and Southeast Asia—but the truth is, nobody knows for sure. If you want to see a really ancient Aby, there's a stuffed one from the 1830s in a Dutch museum (no picture, thank goodness).

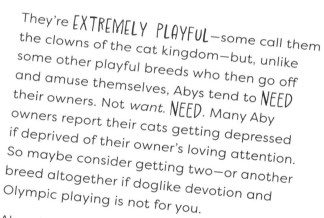

They're EXTREMELY PLAYFUL—some call them the clowns of the cat kingdom—but, unlike some other playful breeds who then go off and amuse themselves, Abys tend to NEED their owners. Not *want*. NEED. Many Aby owners report their cats getting depressed if deprived of their owner's loving attention. So maybe consider getting two—or another breed altogether if doglike devotion and Olympic playing is not for you.

Abys do have a nice quiet meow though. So if they're crying at you for being an awful owner and ignoring them, at least it's done politely.

INTELLIGENCE:	8
PLAYFULNESS:	9
NEEDINESS:	6
OUTDOOR SKILLS:	6
LOVINGNESS:	6

Bengal

Overview

Do you have a WILD RELATIVE who you feel is more like a cave person than a regular human? I do. My Uncle Darren. Although well into his fifties, he still leaps and plays, argues and shouts, and runs about generally being quite wild—particularly if his soccer team are playing. When he's calm though, he's sweet and friendly but wants to talk ALL THE TIME. It just so happens that is more or less the Bengal cat too. Closer to a WILDCAT than most other breeds, the Bengal is actually a charming gentle friend. All its truly wild traits are long gone.

The Bengal was originally bred from the Asian leopard cat. Throw in a smidge of Abyssinian, a teaspoon of Burmese, and a sprinkling of Egyptian Mau—and, voilà, you've got yourself a FEISTY, FUN, PLAYFUL unique cat who also (what a surprise!) has the jungle spot markings of a wildcat.

Personality

As their heritage suggests, the Bengal has a mix of wild, leaping, super-playful characteristics and nuzzling, needy, human-loving tendencies. Could the Bengal be the *most* playful breed? Many say yes. Once you've trained this doglike cat to fetch, they will play for *hours*. They don't seem to get bored with playing.

But don't think this spotted mini leopard just wants to throw itself up trees 24/7. They want YOU to play with them. Of course, they might get distracted by a fly and go on a mega quest, hunting it until sunset—but mostly they will use their (quite loud—be warned!) meow to let you know: "YO! I'M BORED!" Or: "YO! I'M HUNGRY!"

HISTORY

The Bengal was created by breeders who wanted to make a mini leopard. They succeeded! Jean Mill in the USA got things going in the early 1960s, crossing an Asian leopard cat with a domestic shorthair cat.

By the time we reach the summer of love in 1967, the Bengal Love Fest was already in motion. Lots of cross-breeding back and forth occurred, sometimes with a few other breeds—and before long the Bengal breed was what breeders call "true." That means when a male and female have babies, all the babies come out as perfect, full Bengals. It took nearly thirty years for the breed to be officially recognized, but since then . . . people who own Bengals LOVE THEM.

These aren't cats who will lie around looking pretty and leopardy. Definitely not. These are full-on play machines that stay lively well into their older years. They're not really cuddle cats or lap cats either—but it's not because they don't adore their humans. It's just that everything is *too darn interesting!*

Bengals LOVE their family. They LOVE dogs. They LOVE other cats; they LOVE raindrops and flowers and string. You get the picture . . . But they do require proper handling and training early on. No one needs an overly feisty Bengal in their life. So, find an excellent breeder who knows the health and temperament of their cats, and also their history. Some countries do not even allow the ownership of a Bengal, as they class it as a "wild hybrid," so do CHECK your country's laws and regulations.

INTELLIGENCE:	**9**
PLAYFULNESS:	**10**
NEEDINESS:	**8**
OUTDOOR SKILLS:	**8**
LOVINGNESS:	**9**

 CAT BREED
Birman

Overview

This semi-long-haired stunner is a real *catwalk* good-looking cat. Originally named the SACRED CAT of Burma, its flowing silky hair (which does need a bit of grooming) comes in a variety of achingly cute "pointed" colors (meaning that they have a pale body but darker face and tail).

The Birman is a nice blend of friendly, interested, and affectionate—with plenty of easygoing vibes thrown in. Could this be *the* ULTIMATE COMPANION CAT? Have a two-hour cuddle with one purring away like a diesel power generator . . . and you'll probably answer yes!

Personality

Speak to a Birman owner. Many describe these as having the *perfect* temperament. Whereas Ragdolls can be a little too laaaiiiddd-back—and Burmese can be just a touch too needy—the Birman borrows from both these types of energy to become a chilled-out CUDDLE MONSTER who is also obsessed with its family. The only negative thing a few owners have reported is that some Birmans often pick a favorite human—but they still love everyone else too. As with all pets, proper socialization will help with this trait.

HISTORY

The Maine Coon is the oldest truly American breed, originating in the US state of—you guessed it!—Maine. They've been around for two hundred years. The first settlers used them to keep farms and barns clear of massive rats. Over the years, their hunting ability was selectively bred along with hyper-friendliness. They made it to the UK in 1984. The first Maine Coons must have gasped at the tiny British houses and cars: *"Hey, man . . . ONLY have four bedrooms and one stable? That is so weird, dude!"*

These days, Maine Coons are one of the world's most popular breeds. They also make excellent full-body warmers if you can persuade one to lie on you . . .

Maine Coons get along with everyone—from Granny to toddler, to dog, to other cats. They even get along WITH WATER. A paddling Maine Coon is not a rare sight.

Like the idea of a friendly giant in your home? Maine Coon it is, then.

INTELLIGENCE: 8
PLAYFULNESS: 8
NEEDINESS: 6
OUTDOOR SKILLS: 10
LOVINGNESS: 7

Munchkin

Overview

I bet you could have guessed this book would feature a sausage-shaped dog . . . but a SAUSAGE CAT? Ladies and gentlemen, I give you . . . the Munchkin!

Not everyone is a fan of the Munchkin (its name comes from *The Wonderful Wizard of Oz*). Some call it the sausage cat. I am a fan. It's a sausage-shaped cat—of course I am—but the fact is that some countries' official cat-breeding associations do not recognize the Munchkin. I don't mean they look away and pretend not to see it. What I mean is, they don't count it as an official breed. Some say that it is cruel to breed cats with stubby legs, while others argue that the breed occurred naturally (it did) so they are just following what nature started. Either way, the Munchkin is VERY popular. If you're thinking of getting one, it's important that you do your research very carefully and speak to a breeder.

Also, with legs the size of BABY CARROTS, it makes cat-proofing the yard a lot simpler. I'm guessing that whittling (sharpening claws) will still occur . . . just much lower down the sofa . . .

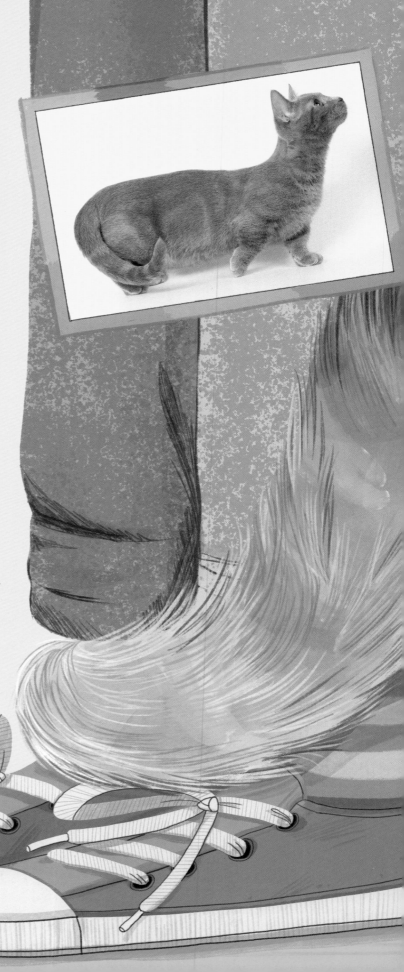

HISTORY

Cats with short legs have occurred multiple times in the past century. Interestingly, it appears to be a similar genetic mutation that makes Dachshunds have short legs . . . That reminds me, I must sequence my Uncle Keith's DNA—he could be the first miniature uncle breed ever recorded.

It was a lady in Louisiana, USA (the home of BIG things, confusingly), who found a couple of stray sausage cats and thought, *Hey, this could be a brand-new breed, but what will we call these little munchkins? . . . Darn it . . . That's it—the Munchkin!*

And that is the mini history of the mini-legged mini cat named the Munchkin.

Personality

The Munchkin has been selected for its distinctive LOOK rather than its personality—you don't always get both.* Most Munchkin lovers talk about how the cat moves rather than its temperament. They move like FERRETS slinking around and do little baby jumps when they get excited.

Saying that, it's an even-tempered cat—friendly, curious, intelligent, and affectionate. They are very bright too and will need lots of stimulation and games. The main personality that will be affected, however, is yours . . . when you turn to goo watching a sausage with whiskers play with a toy mouse.

INTELLIGENCE: **7**
PLAYFULNESS: **6**
NEEDINESS: **5**
OUTDOOR SKILLS: **1**
LOVINGNESS: **8**

*Unlike me. (Pouts in mirror for ten solid minutes.)

Persian

Overview

The Persian cat has been a breed for almost a thousand years. Originating in Iran, these FLUFFY BALLS of loveliness (although you can get a short-haired version named an Exotic Shorthair too) are one of the most famous and ancient of all the cat breeds.

If you're considering adopting one in any of its array of colors . . . then think of the Persian as the OPPOSITE of, say, a Siamese. If a Siamese is your needy, moany, but fun friend from school who *always* has to have someone to play with, then the Persian cat is like your AUNTIE who doesn't like to be startled and is quite happy to have a cup of tea on her own with a good book. (Though I'm not suggesting your auntie poops in a litter tray, by the way.)

HISTORY

Some say that the long-haired cats featured in ancient hieroglyphs were the first Persian cats . . . If this is true, it would make them the most ancient of all the cat breeds, not man-made but naturally emerging. They were named Persians because people thought that the breed had started in Iran, which used to be named Persia.

Swish forward to 1871, and we *do* know that the very first EVER big cat show in London had Persians. Not only that but Queen Victoria loved them. And if she liked something, then BABE—IT WAS SO ON TREND! No wonder the Persian went on to become one of the most popular breeds ALL over the world.

Personality

Loyal, loving, affectionate . . . and more CHILLED than a bottle of cola on a summer's day, the Persian is an excellent all-arounder. They won't nag or scream at you; they won't try to do show-off stunt climbing like eighteen-year-olds on their first foreign holiday without Mom and Dad. They won't demand anything much.

They LOVE CUDDLES, and they will adore their owners—it's just that they're quite happy watching the world tick by through a sun-drenched window looking on to the street. They make excellent indoor-only cats.

While they get along well with all the family—including dogs—they are by no means like a Ragdoll. A Persian will let you know if you've crossed its boundary, so WELL BEHAVED and GENTLE children are best. (I was neither of those things . . . so no judgment here!)

INTELLIGENCE: **7**
PLAYFULNESS: **4**
NEEDINESS: **3**
OUTDOOR SKILLS: **3**
LOVINGNESS: **9**

Dogs

There is no other domestic pet on the planet that will give you that one-on-one love like a dog. I say "domestic" because some people genuinely keep chimpanzees. I would not recommend this as it is (A) illegal, and (B) they can get really big and then starting throwing poop around the house and fighting outside. Admittedly this describes my Uncle Darren too . . . but he, sadly, was still legal at time of writing.

The dog is a full member of the family. Their intelligence is amazing. They are not smarter than cats . . . it's just that they are more willing to do what YOU want them to do with their intelligence. I'm yet to see a guide cat for blind people—though, as a Burmese cat owner, I would not rule it out.

It's really important that you know the temperament of any dog or puppy. If you're getting a rescue dog, try to find out as much of its history as possible, and be prepared to put the time into the training. If you're getting a puppy, DO NOT CHOOSE THE FIRST PUPPY THAT RUNS TOWARD YOU . . . unless you actually want the most dominant and excitable puppy in the litter. Neither should you select the scared, shivering, cute puppy . . . Try to get a nice middle-of-the-road puppy in the litter. That is likely to become the most level-headed adult dog. If you don't believe me, think about the craziest, most energy-filled person in your class. Now imagine hanging out with them in twenty years' time . . . See what I mean?

If you are getting a pedigree dog, it's super important to select a breed that is appropriate for you and your family. Yeah, a Springer Spaniel might have the love-pool eyes and floppy ears you want, but in the winter is anyone in the family really going to head out for a one-hour walk with them? Thought not. Think about ENERGY and TEMPERAMENT and SIZE before anything else.

Right! Here are my favorite breeds . . .

Border Collie

Overview

Do you have a friend or a relative who always has to be working? They hate vacations, and they're always boasting about how many hours of homework they've done even after tennis and pottery club . . . ? Well, that's exactly what the Border Collie is like. Super bright (some say the brightest), super hard-working, and super, super sociable—the Border Collie is a dog that must have something to do ALL day EVERY DAY.

Do not dare even read another sentence if you live in the city and your family lead a busy life away from home . . . If that's the case, the Border Collie is not for you, I promise!

Personality

Widely regarded as one of the most iNTELLiGENT dogs on earth, the Border Collie learns quickly and loves to help out. I've not tried it myself, but I'd love to let them give some math homework a try. Border Collies were bred to herd . . . and they HERD EVERYTHiNG: sheep, cars, and even you—so it's essential they have someone to be with during the day, so they can stay "tasked up." Even if you have a MASSIVE yard, it won't be enough. They need one-on-one walking and things to do, otherwise they'll invent their own hobbies like chasing cats and ruining furniture.

54

HISTORY

You probably already know that Border Collies were bred to herd sheep. And that was a lonnnng time ago in the 1700s. You may have also figured out that the breed was developed on the borders of Scotland and England. But, as with much of history, it was rich people who made them popular. And in the nineteenth century Queen Victoria was the fanciest old woman on the planet and it was SHE who made Border Collies popular forever. Like a Kardashian drinking a Pepsi instead of a Coca-Cola. In those days, they were just named collies, but they got their proper name, Border Collies, in 1915 by a guy in the International Sheep Dog Society who wanted to differentiate between the different collie breeds. That is some dog-breed nerd info for you right there!

Although Border Collies are good with children they know, they might be a bit funny with strangers—even nipping heels and HERDING GUESTS. This sounds great to me . . . but most people don't enjoy it. A massive amount of training is required. Maybe send your puppy to Oxford University to do . . . a master's degree in DOG-GRAPHY. That way they'll know you're the boss. (That was way too many words for a very bad joke.)

They LOVE their family and make excellent guard dogs, constantly on alert and listening out for any strange noises. This also means they are extra sensitive to noise, so they're not fans of firework nights. (I know, the loud ones make me piddle just a little, too.)

INTELLIGENCE: **11**
PLAYFULNESS: **10**
NEEDINESS: **10**
OUTDOOR SKILLS: **10**
LOVINGNESS: **5**

HISTORY

There's a reason why they're sausage-shaped and a reason why they have "Dachs" in their name. Hundreds of years ago, Dachshunds were bred to wriggle down holes and chase out badgers—and Dachs is German for "badger," so their name literally means "badger dog." (Yup, hund is German for "dog.") This also explains their determined and sometimes stubborn nature. If I'm gonna hire someone to dig a hole for me, I want them to stick to it. The wieners became more and more popular through the nineteenth century all the way through to today . . . Wiener Dog Love Fest . . .

Dachshunds are fierce, loyal, protective, and stubborn, but they have a CLOWNISH side too. They'll toss toys at your feet, gaze at you comically—and they hate being bored. Give them something to dig . . . and they'll dig it.

Early training is essential, especially if there are small children in your family, so a lot of patience is needed with them. All that said, my mom's Connie is one of the gentlest, most affectionate souls I've ever stroked (unless you count my house rabbit Barbara—see "Rabbits," page 94-95). Some Dachshunds can be yappy yet Connie is mute, so maybe check with the breeder and see what the parents are like.

INTELLIGENCE: **8**
PLAYFULNESS: **7**
NEEDINESS: **6**
OUTDOOR SKILLS: **9**
LOVINGNESS: **8**

 DOG BREED

French Bulldog

Overview

Bred to be a miniature bulldog, these toy-sized, BAT-PIG, pointy-eared clowns have long lost any urge to fight with bulls and cattle. I have a pug named Colin—and I always think of French Bulldogs as like Pugs who have had a makeover. Slightly less farty, smelly, and wheezy—with a bit more energy.

They're an excellent all-rounder dog, but they do need someone to train them properly and let them know that the humans are in charge and not the Frenchies . . .

Personality

You immediately smile when you see a French Bulldog. And so you should—these barrel-bellied JOKERS go out of their way to be the center of games and fun in the middle of any household. Frenchies love zooming around, throwing toys in the air like someone put double-strength coffee in their water bowl. If the toy hits your TV, they'll turn around and look at you as if to say, "Didn't I do good?" They are SILLY but also BRAVE. A Frenchie will normally let you know if someone's at the door—they might need to sniff and lick a visitor into submission, after all . . .

They also ADORE food. Do not overfeed a Frenchie, otherwise you will no longer have a miniature bulldog. You will simply have a dog double the size, so . . . a bulldog.

HISTORY

People argue a bit about where Frenchies come from—but most agree: not France! I know, right? There is a reason though. Back in the 1800s everyone really loved LACE. I mean, lace was like the Pokémon of the day. And Nottingham in England was the best at making it. The Notts lace makers, who worked from home, loved miniature English Bulldogs: they chased away rats and didn't take up too much room. So, when factories took over, and the lace makers packed up and took their skills to France, they took their mini dogs with them. And, of course, the French fell in love with these dinky canines—and that is how the French Bulldog came about. To keep lace makers company. (I never would have guessed that either. Good quiz knowledge to have . . .) The breed did change a bit in France with the inclusion of other breeds.

They've got squashed faces and are very popular at the moment—but that means there might be some unhealthy ones out there, so PLEASE find an excellent breeder with a proper website and the correct credentials.

Frenchies are excellent family dogs, but they do need guidance and training when they are pups. I remember at my pug Colin's puppy classes it was always the Pugs, Boxers, and Frenchies who were the most STUBBORN in learning to walk on a leash. Frenchies are bright—and they know too darn well what a leash is . . . just make sure they learn! "POURQUOI?" they will say. "WHY SHOULD I?"

INTELLIGENCE: 5
PLAYFULNESS: 9
NEEDINESS: 7
OUTDOOR SKILLS: 5
LOVINGNESS: 8

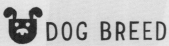 DOG BREED

Jack Russell Terrier

Overview

My whole life, people have told me that I have an unusual amount of ENERGY; that I am "exhausting"; that one day I will "burn out" that energy and fall asleep in the corner eating pretzels. Well, guess what. I have more energy than ever. Luckily, discovering comedy has given me my own daily "hamster wheel." When I pick up that microphone and run around for ninety minutes, shouting grown-up words at drunk grown-ups . . . all my energy is expended, and then I'm ready to curl up in my bed with a tasty treat, normally a chicken kebab. OK, so am I talking about Russell Kane or Jack Russell . . . ? Because we seem to be the same creature, and with that much energy we are DEFINITELY NOT for people who like a quiet life.

I would say if you don't have a yard, DO NOT get a Jack Russell. Or if you already have small pets like hamsters, gerbils, birds or small cats.

Personality

The Jack Russell may look like a compact terrier—it is—but in that little body is a POWERHOUSE of running, jumping, digging, and hunting. Most of the breeds in this book can be trained thoroughly so that their original instincts are dialed down a bit. Not the Jack Russell . . . Even if you sent it to the Royal College of Sitting Down for ten years, it would run out of the exit, dig a hole, then try to catch a squirrel. These mighty pooches were bred to hunt and they need AT LEAST one to two hours of exercise EVERY DAY if you want a well-behaved doggy. If you're a sporting family . . . then a Jack Russell might be the dog for you. #Frisbee

HISTORY

The Schnauzer, as well as being hard to spell (trust me, I know—I'm writing this chapter), is one of the oldest German breeds. Rumor has it that the original Standard Schnauzer was created by crossing a Poodle with a Gray Wolfspitz (a domestic breed descended from wild dogs), probably in the fourteenth century.

There is a bit of a debate about whether these dogs were terriers or working dogs. You could argue that the Miniatures are more terrier-like and the Standards and Giants are a bit more "worky." After all, Schnauzers were bred to run into barns and tell the rodents, "I don't want any trouble, pal . . . But you need to move out." They also helped in German farmers' markets, herding creatures right up until the World War I.

For me, they are a bit of both terrier and working dog. Maybe I'll get a Schnauzer and he can clean the yard for me, then pop to the store to pick up some veggies. Yeah . . . I like the sound of that . . .

And if you have neighbors who are a bit whiny, consider that Schnauzers love to bark. I mean, they want to tell you about EVERYTHING! "Mom/Dad! A leaf just moved three streets away—mind if I bark like I've lost my mind for a few minutes?" That'll do, Schnauzie . . .

A good walk each day will help drain that Schnauzer energy. Oh, and if you keep rabbits or gerbils, beware . . . The name Schnauzer comes from the German word Schnauz, which means "snout," because these dogs were bred to stick their noses into holes and rip apart rodents and rabbits—so they might not be a good housemate for Thumper.

INTELLIGENCE: 9
PLAYFULNESS: 7
NEEDINESS: 9
OUTDOOR SKILLS: 10
LOVINGNESS: 8

DOG BREED
Shih Tzu

Overview

I loved these compact little beauties when I was little—not because I wanted one but because my mom couldn't yell at me for saying their name. Sadly, she looked up the correct way to pronounce it, which is "SHEEEEE TSU"—and so not like the swear word I had been using.

The reason this awesome little dog is in this book? It's because they are AWESOME. Yes, they have long flowing hair like they have joined a heavy metal band—which means they require lots of grooming . . . but they are so worth it.

HISTORY

The Sheeeeeeeee Ta-zuuu (keep practicing so you don't get in trouble like I did when I was eight) has a long and noble royal history. They've been named LION DOGS for centuries—Shih Tzu means "little lion" in Mandarin Chinese. They were bred originally to follow Buddhist monks and Chinese royalty around the palace, just for companionship. Not many dogs have PURE FRIENDSHIP in their pedigree.

Sometimes the doggies slept in the billowing sleeves of royal folk—or even in the bed as bed warmers. I hope the owners trained those dogs well . . . or it wouldn't just be fur warming that royal forearm. And the bed might smell a little funny too—of POOOO TZU!

Personality

Short, sturdy, full of love, and always wanting to be with people . . . No, not my Uncle Keith but the lovely little Shih Tzu. They are TEENY and FRIENDLY—and adore cuddling. They also love to learn. Although it is a bit comical to watch a dog with a bow in its hair do an agility course, Shih Tzus are actually super bright and good in the show ring. These are not dogs who can be left alone though. They love their humans; they love children too.

My only word of caution: the Shih Tzu, like my nephew Barnaby, could be the most SPOILABLE creature on the planet. They are so cute, with such floppy hair and adoring eyes, that they get EASILY spoiled. And spoiled = snappy. And snappy = a trip to the doctor for a tetanus shot if your hand gets snapped at.

Whatever you do with these awesome all-arounders, TRAIN THEM PROPERLY. If you do, you will have one of the best dogs you'll ever know. My wife, Lindsey, comes from a home that had two Shih Tzus—Tess and Candy—and her whole family still talks about them to this day.

INTELLIGENCE: 7
PLAYFULNESS: 6
NEEDINESS: 8
OUTDOOR SKILLS: 4
LOVINGNESS: 8

DOG BREED
Staffordshire Bull Terrier

Overview

What do you get if you cross a BODYBUiLDER with a HiPPiE? A Staffordshire Bull Terrier! They are chunky, muscly, and tough-looking. Indeed, they might look like pirates who've just arrived to loot your gold and chew your leg but guess what? They are literally one of the GENTLEST breeds with families and children. Some even argue that Staffies PREFER children to grown-ups. Of course, no dog should EVER be left unattended with small children, but the Staffy's reputation as a nurse dog is well known.

How could a breed descended from nineteenth-century fighting dogs have become such a lover rather than a fighter? The answer is simple: They've been living closely with families for a hundred years. Although they must still be VERY CAREFULLY trained and socialized (or you'll have a difficult dog on your hands), they are a long way from their roots.

Personality

It's a shame that the Staffy has the look of a mean alleyway brawler about to take on a bare-knuckle fight where the winner gets a pile of sausages . . . because all they want to do is hang out and cuddle. Of course, an ALERT and CHEERFUL dog like this loves walking, but they also love gently panting next to you while you watch ten hours of Netflix straight through.

Being honest, I met some people in show business who've had **LESS** personality than my stick insect, Rambo. And my ex-girlfriend Samantha certainly became scarier than a wasp when I suggested that our love was over. By the way, Samantha—can I please have **ALL** my pants back? Why did you take them?

More important than anything though, when considering an insect . . . is the stuff you'll need. Man! you're going to need a lot. Use the internet or even better, **A BOOKSHOP** or **LIBRARY**, to find out about the particular stuff you need for your type of insect—but I will tell you right now it can be expensive (vivariums, lights, and so on). Also, they take up more space than you think they'll need, and most vitally (from a parent's point of view) . . . insects stink a fair bit. It's not something you'd guess by looking at them, but crickets, for example. **POOOOOWEEEEE!** They do smell! In fact, they could definitely use a tiny deodorant stick under each of their amazing, musical legs.*

Whichever insect you go for—enjoy it! Abandon yourself to the research— and do let me know how it goes.

INTELLIGENCE: **4**
PLAYFULNESS: **1**
NEEDINESS: **1**
OUTDOOR SKILLS: **10**
LOVINGNESS: **2**

*Please don't ever attempt to put deodorant on any creature—that includes my Auntie Caroline, who only does "natural" and "organic" and won't wear ANY deodorant and therefore smells of potatoes.

OTHER PETS
Rodents

Mice, gerbils, guinea pigs, hamsters, rats . . .
No, this isn't the start of a witch's (my nana's)
spell but these are genuinely rewarding pets
if cared for properly. Not everyone can give
up their home to an animal, so an animal
that lives in some sort of enclosure might
be the answer.

I think the most important thing is to make
sure they have enough SPACE for them to be
happy. Whichever rodent you go for, there are
loads of internet resources and books aplenty
that will tell you how to care for that animal,
and all the stuff you'll need.

IMPORTANT NOTE: not all rodents have the
same vibe.

My brother's mouse, Ivy, was adorable—but,
if I'm being honest, she was a bit BORING.
She slept a lot, then now and again she ran
on her wheel. I suppose it was quite special
to cuddle and stroke her, and her twitching
nose melted our hearts. It's the same with
gerbils. My niece had a gerbil named
Shazam. We tried everything to make him as
exciting as possible—making up stories for
him, giving him awesome agility tests to do—
but he was a little on the sleepy side.

Guinea pigs are bigger and more commitment but A LOT more fun. They give more back and dart around grunting like furry little rodent clowns. As well as that, they don't mind being petted and have a bit more personality.

But—and your mom, dad, granny, sister and brother will not thank me for this—when it comes to the most interesting, most awesome, most interactive and loving rodent buddy, there's no competition. It's the RAT!

Rats are super bright and gentle, and—if raised properly (yes, there are AWESOME RAT BREEDERS) by someone who knows what they are doing—they make AMAZING pets for people who can't have dogs or cats. You even get different types, and the Dumbo Rat is said to be the friendliest. Males tend to be more chilled than females. But all breeder-reared rats can be loving. I'm talking games, belly rubs, head scratches, and full cuddles. I know, I know . . . you're reading this screaming "PLAGUE!" but, trust me, ditch your prejudice and head to a bookshop, library, or the internet to find out more about rats as pets and see for yourself. Rats are amazing. Ugly teeth though.

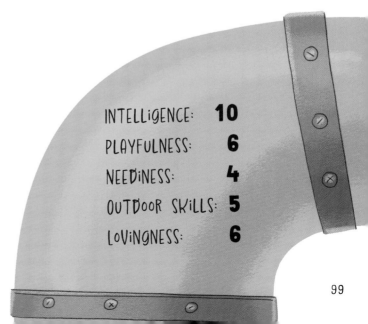

INTELLIGENCE: **10**
PLAYFULNESS: **6**
NEEDINESS: **4**
OUTDOOR SKILLS: **5**
LOVINGNESS: **6**

Budgies

I was going to include a general section on birds, but on reflection (in my budgie mirror) I'd prefer to just tell you about the (seemingly) humble budgie. Here's why.

Most importantly, these birds have been domesticated for over TWO HUNDRED YEARS. They take well to being in a house—much better than trying to force some wild African bird to live in a city apartment or suburban house. Secondly, their size makes them an ideal pet—trying to keep a large bird in a small home is worse than my massive Uncle Tony trying to fit into an aeroplane middle seat. Yes, they need a bit of daily wing-stretching exercise (two hours, ideally), but they are small birds, so they are easier to keep happy . . . or should that be "chirpy"? And, finally, they actually seem to ENJOY home life. I don't speak budgie, but I'm reliably informed that they do indeed like human company too. Or as they would say: PEEP, TWAAARP, BRRP, BRRR.

They do NOT enjoy cat company though. Really, it should go without saying that you shouldn't combine this pet with a resident cat. You might as well get some garnish and chips if you're planning on doing that!

Regarding equipment, do some research on all the stuff you'll need. It's quite a bit: cages, toys, food, and so on. There's more to think about than you might, well, think. And remember: these sturdy little birds can live for nearly a decade. You'll be king driving lessons when they are still pecking at their millet.

This is the only time in this book you will read these words, but consider getting JUST ONE pet budgie. At least at first. Budgies form strong bonds with their families—but if you get two babies at the same time, they tend to bond with each other, and you won't get that awesome human-budgie interaction. You'd be better off getting one, then maybe a few months later getting a companion budgie and socializing that budgie separately, in another room. Once you have two adult budgies who love you and speak human, introduce them to each other, very carefully, in a NEUTRAL space—so a third cage or one of the original cages sterilized clean. Then hey presto! You'll have two birdies who love you, but who won't get lonely if you can't give them all the attention they need.

Did I mention about not mixing them with cats? Thought that was worth saying twice . . .

Do not think that because your tiny birdie has a tiny head, that it has a tiny brain. NO! Budgies are extremely bright and affectionate. They can recognize voices and faces, learn to hum little tunes and nestle lovingly in your hands. They are actually a type of parrot. So all this nonsense about a budgie not being as good as a parrot is exactly that: poppycock (which sounds like a bird, confusingly)! A budgie is a full parrot with a full parrott-y brain.

INTELLIGENCE:	11
PLAYFULNESS:	7
NEEDINESS:	8
OUTDOOR SKILLS:	0
LOVINGNESS:	5

OTHER PETS
Reptiles

Finally, reptiles. I wasn't sure whether to include them—after all, this book is about temperament and personality, and owning a reptile is more about the physical and maybe the learning experience, rather than the emotions. That said, I formed quite a bond with my garter snake, Oscar. Feeding him earthworms and crickets was REALLY exciting (not for the crickets, I admit) . . . Yes, he may not have had much personality, but it was a real thrill watching him shed his old snake skin and slither around hunting for unlucky insects. He would also curl up in my palm, flicking his tongue at me and tasting the air.

There is also a fair amount of cost to think about: a vivarium (special glass container that can be sealed), heated lamps, special bedding and food . . . Also, newsflash: reptiles do massive poops. At one stage I had three tortoises (please DO NOT get a pet tortoise) named Sally, Hilda, and Bumper—and Bumper's poops were bigger than my Yorkshire Terrier Barney's. Tortoises are incredibly complicated to look after and, sadly, we ended up rehoming all three of ours. Some people are for tortoise-owning; others are against it. Dig deeper and do a bit more research.

Maybe you are the right person to get a gecko, bearded dragon, or a snake, but think long and hard about it, and DO YOUR RESEARCH. How big will it grow? What equipment will you need? Can you even touch and cuddle your new pet? Also, if you don't like watching animals eaten alive, then definitely don't get a reptile . . . You might find that behavior hard to swallow. Sorry.

INTELLIGENCE: 4
PLAYFULNESS: 1
NEEDINESS: 2
OUTDOOR SKILLS: 2
LOVINGNESS: 1

Conclusion

I hope you enjoyed my pet personality guide. This book is not a substitute for proper information about care and rearing and grooming and all that stuff. There are loads of really good books on the technical business of pet ownership and, if I'm being completely honest, I found it way too much hard work to look it up and do a bunch of research. I do FUN for a job, so I have brought to life the fun part of choosing a pet . . . "What will my new pal BE LIKE?" A pet can be so much more than a furry (or bald) creature to look after. It can become a best friend, a comfort when you're down or even someone to chat to . . . I swear my maggot Brian used to listen. If you end up loving animals enough . . . who knows? You might, like me, end up writing a book about the joy of it!

Anyway, can you guess what I'm going to do with some of my pocket money from making this fun book? Well, put it this way, I've already contacted a Savannah cat breeder . . . I'm feeling another fur baby coming on. WAHHHHHH!

Breeders

I've mentioned it a few times but I'll turn into a teacher now and SAY IT AGAIN. Please use BREEDERS who really know their stuff. They know how to raise and handle your new pet, and they will be bursting with expert tips and advice too. If you want to hunt for excellent breeders or just get more information I've included some useful links here too.

* **Cats UK** www.gccfcats.org
* **Cats USA** www.cfa.org/ and www.acfacat.com
* **Dogs UK** www.thekennelclub.org.uk
* **Dogs USA** www.akc.org

Animal-proofing

There are excellent books and online resources about preparing your home for a new pet, but I just want to mention that it's important to cat/dog/rabbit-proof your home if you don't want your new cat/dog/rabbit (or other animal) to chew and scratch everything in sight and within reach once you bring it home. Young (and older) cats and dogs will be tempted to use chair and table legs for whittling (to sharpen their claws) so make sure that your parents protect any valuable furniture!

For cats and dogs who might want to play in the yard, take time to research whether you must escape-proof your yard (and what you need to do if you do need to escape-proof it). Some cat breeds are waaaay too innocent and friendly to leave the safety of your yard—this is something very important to bear in mind. Could you make your yard cat-proof? Could you build a cat enclosure? What about the special collars that cats (and dogs) can wear so that they cannot leave the boundary of your home? Mostly, with cats, it's simpler just to have house cats and a litter tray. Speak to breeders: they really are so very excellent at knowing their own breed.

Saint Isidora

A Fool for Christ

Feast Day: May 1

Whatever people expected, Isidora did the opposite. Instead of wanting people to think that she was beautiful or clever or holy, she hid herself by acting like a fool. Isidora was a nun who lived in Egypt, but she was not like the other nuns. Instead of wearing a veil over her hair, she wore a dirty dishrag. When everyone else wore sandals, she went barefoot. She wouldn't eat meals with the other sisters and they thought she was crazy.

Isidora took on the most difficult jobs in monastery. She worked in the kitchen and even though no one liked her, she was always kind. In her heart, she loved God and her sisters and worked to serve them. When she heard people saying bad things about her, she remained silent and prayed for them.

One day, an angel visited a monk named Saint Pitrim. The angel told Pitrim to leave the desert and find someone who was more holy than him, so God lead Pritrim to Isidora's monastery. When he arrived, all of the nuns greeted Pitrim, but he could tell that the holy woman was not with them. When he asked about anyone else, someone answered that only the fool was missing.

When Isidora was brought out, Pitrim bowed before her. The other nuns were amazed, but he revealed her kindness and holiness. Now that the others knew her secret, Isidora ran away. She did not want fame or honor, only to love God.

A Prayer:

O Holy Saint Isidora, pray that we will not worry about what others think of us and only care about pleasing our Lord Jesus Christ. Amen.

Saint Dymphna

Patron Saint of those suffering from nervous or mental afflictions

Feast Day: May 15

There was once an Irish princess named Dymphna whose mother was the most beautiful woman in the land. Dymphna's mother was a devout Christian who loved Jesus even though her husband still worshiped the old pagan gods of Ireland. When her mother died, Dymphna knew that she would see her again in heaven. Her father, however, was desperate. As he mourned for his beautiful wife, his mind became sick and twisted until everyone around him knew he needed help.

The king's advisors suggested he remarry and so the king agreed, with one condition. He would only marry a woman as beautiful as his late wife. The search went out but as many beautiful women were presented to the king, he only wanted someone who looked like his wife. His mind became more and more ill until at last, it was not safe for Dymphna to remain near him She ran from his court to the home of the local priest, Father Gerebernus who helped her flee across the sea to Belgium.

Dymphna settled in the town of Geel and used her fortune to build a hospital for the poor and mentally ill in that area. Unfortunately, her father was able to trace her to Belgium. When he and his soldiers came for her, Dymphna was only 15 years old. The king ordered that the soldiers kill the kindly priest and demanded that Dymphna return to Ireland with him. She refused and in his anger, he drew his sword and cut off her head.

Saint Dymphna's relics are venerated in the town of Geel, where her sanctuary for the mentally ill still provides healing for people today.

A Prayer:

O Dymphna, you healed many bodies and minds. Comfort me when I am worried. Calm my mind when I am afraid. Pray to God for me that I will think clearly and that I will have your love for people whose minds are ill.

Saint Sunniva

Patron Saint of Western Norway

Feast Day: July 8

Sunniva had to run away. A neighboring king who refused to follow God wanted to marry her. Even though St. Patrick had come to Ireland nearly 500 years before, there were still some people who chose to follow the old gods. Sunniva's fiancé was one of these people and she knew that it would be wrong to marry him. When she refused his offer, he invaded her family's kingdom. She had nothing left to do but run.

Late in the night, Sunniva, her brother and some others boarded a ship and left Ireland. They sailed across the sea but were shipwrecked on a small island off the coast of Norway. Huddled in a cave, the siblings were happy to be together and thankful that God had brought them to a new land.

Sunniva and her companions lived peacefully in the cave but soon there was trouble again. The people of the island suspected them of stealing sheep and sent for the local ruler. Sunniva prayed to God that they should not be captured by the unbelievers and rocks fell down and blocked the cave entrance.

Years later, the Christian king, Olaf Tryggvason, heard reports of strange lights and miracles in the area and ordered the cave opened. Sunniva's body was found inside and it had not decayed. The king built a Church in her honor and Saint Sunniva was canonized as the first saint of Norway.

A Prayer:

Let us rejoice in your holiness, O Saint Sunniva. Seas, waves and islands rejoice because you loved and served God. Pray that we will do the same.

Saint Margaret of Antioch

Patron Saint of childbirth, pregnant women and kidney diseases.

Feast Day: July 20 or July 17

Margaret (who is also called Marina) grew up without a mother. Her father was a pagan priest who couldn't care for her so he gave her into the care of a nursemaid who loved and raised Margaret as her own. As the child grew, the nurse taught Margaret the Christian faith in secret. But, when she was 15 years old, her father discovered her secret faith and disowned her. Margaret and her nurse went to live in the country and Margaret became a shepherd.

One day, the governor, Olymbrios, saw how beautiful Margaret was and tried to convince her to deny her Christian faith and marry him. Over and over, Margaret refused him until he became angry and ordered that she be arrested and tortured for her faith. She was beaten and burned and encountered a demon in the form of a dragon. When the soldiers tried to drown her, a dove appeared from Heaven and brought Margaret a golden crown. She emerged from the water, completely healed and wearing the crown forged by faith.

When the people saw how God saved Margaret, they were amazed and believed in Christ. The governor was so angry that he ordered that anyone who said that Jesus was God would be killed. Over 15,000 people became martyrs and Margaret was finally beheaded.

A Prayer:

O Saint Margaret, you gave up everything to follow Christ! Pray for me to be like you that I may serve God, no matter what stands in my way.